Sun Moon Star

Kurt Vonnegut
Ivan Chermayeff

Harper & Row, Publishers

Behold,
a virgin shall be with child,
and shall bring forth a son,
and they shall call his name Emanuel,
which being interpreted is,
God with us.

Sun Moon Star
Text copyright © 1980 by Kurt Vonnegut
Illustrations copyright © 1980 by Ivan Chermayeff
All rights reserved.
No part of this book may be used
or reproduced in any manner whatsoever
without written permission
except in the case of brief quotations
embodied in critical articles and reviews.
Printed in the United States of America.
For information address Harper & Row, Publishers, Inc.,
10 East 53rd Street, New York, N.Y. 10022.
Published simultaneously in Canada
by Fitzhenry & Whiteside Limited, Toronto.
FIRST EDITION

Library of Congress Cataloging in Publication Data
Vonnegut, Kurt.
Sun moon star.

SUMMARY: When the Creator of the universe
came to Earth, It resolved to be born a male human
infant, and this is what It saw when It opened
its eyes.
1. Jesus Christ—Juvenile poetry.
2. Children's poetry, American.   [1. Jesus
Christ—Nativity—Poetry.   2. American poetry]
I. Chermayeff, Ivan.   II. Title.
PS3572.O5S8 1980   811'.54   79-9612
ISBN 0-06-026319-9

To begin:

When the Creator of the Universe
came to Earth,
when It resolved to be born
as a male human infant
in a stable
attached to a busy inn,
It had never had need for eyes before.
It had known all things and been all things.
The Creator had only to exist.
That was enough.
But now, as a human infant,
It was also going to see—
and to do so imperfectly,
through two human eyes,
each a rubbery little camera.

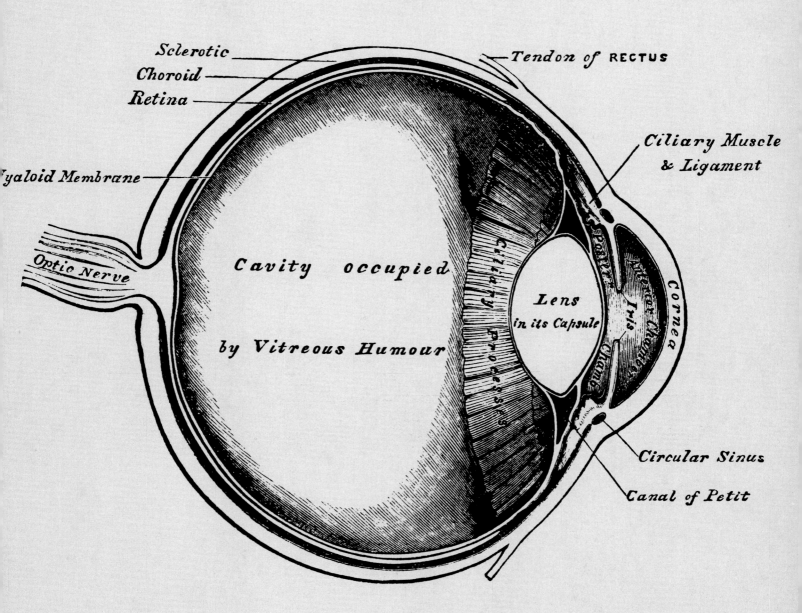

Sclerotic
Choroid
Retina

Tendon of RECTUS

Hyaloid Membrane

Ciliary Muscle
& Ligament

Optic Nerve

Cavity   occupied

Ciliary Processes

by Vitreous Humour

Lens
in its Capsule

Posterior Chamber

Anterior Chamber

Iris

Cornea

Circular Sinus

Canal of Petit

It was night when the Creator was born.
It cried like anyone else.
When It opened Its eyes wide for the first time,
they were filled with tears
and bleary.
It could not see anything
in detail.
It could not tell what was near
and what was far.
Thus did It confuse the flame of a lamp
held near It,
a burning rag in a cup of oil,
with a supernova,
with the exploding
Christmas star.

A crescent moon arose.
The points of the Christmas star
dropped off.
There were cries of dismay.
There were thumps.
Only one minute old,
and cradled in the hands of a midwife,
the Creator had witnessed Its first
human accident.
The moon was the forehead of Joseph,
who would pretend to be the Creator's father
with all his heart.
Joseph held the lamp.
Joseph so adored the infant
that he had allowed the lamp to tilt.
The falling points of the star
were beads of burning oil.
The thumps were made by Joseph's feet
as he stamped out the little fires
on the stable floor.
Joseph begged the forgiveness of God.
He was heard.

The Creator
closed Its eyes tight
for the first time,
expecting to return
to all-knowing darkness.
It learned that perfect darkness
would not be Its again
for so long as It chose to live.
Human eyes, It learned,
imagined that they saw things
even when they were closed.
They showed the Creator
all these imaginary
suns.

The Creator opened Its eyes wide again.
This would be the second time.
The sky was now a dazzling chaos.
It was nothing but exploding
Christmas stars.
A Roman matron, a tourist,
a guest at the inn,
had come into the stable for the amusement
of seeing a baby,
any baby,
born.
She wished to show the baby
something wonderful at once,
and so had removed a crystal necklace
from her throat,
and now dangled
those prismatic chips of quartz, backlit,
before the Creator's eyes.

The necklace was not to be a present.
Only the memory of its
glitter was the Creator's to keep.
The Roman matron
was called back to the inn
by her husband.
All the Christmas stars fled
as the necklace was hastily
withdrawn.
And a seeming sun
began to rise.

The midwife
was now giving the Creator
into the arms of Its mother
Mary.
Mary,
in her radiance
after all the pain was gone,
was the seeming rising
sun.

Mary
was little more
than a child
herself—

But the Creator of the Universe,
unbelievingly and rapturously,
felt all Creation
easily engulfed
and lovingly
by a single
rising sun.

The Creator
closed Its eyes tight for the second time,
and It sucked
warm milk
from
Its mother.

The Creator slept.

It dreamed
Its first dream.

It dreamed
Its second dream.

It dreamed
Its third dream.

Its fourth dream was simply green.
It had never seen
green
before.

It was still night
when It awoke.
It saw this seeming moon,
which was the midwife
keeping watch.

The pale sheen on her face
was lamplight.
Now the lamp was moved
by Joseph,
who wished to look
at the sleeping Mary,
causing the seeming moon
to wane.

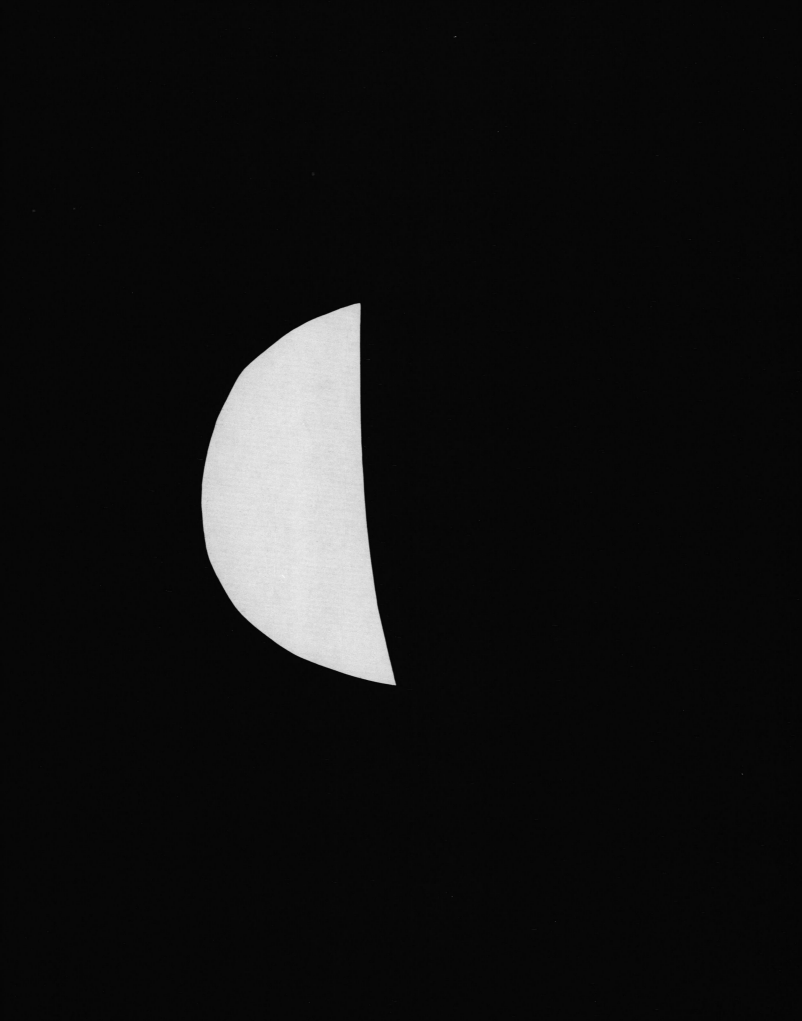

Now the sounds of oceanic alarm
and grief filled the infant's ears.
It was the bleating of sheep
brought down from the hills by shepherds
who were following
what the Creator could not see
from Its manger,
which was the real Christmas star.
Mary was awakened.
She came now and looked down on the Creator
with the midwife,
a seeming sun in partial eclipse
to the Creator,
who could not move a hand or foot,
bound as It was,
a tiny package,
in swaddling clothes.

Yes,

and Mary picked up her baby.

It might be necessary to flee,

as weak as she was.

The King had declared that all newborn male babies

were to be

executed.

She held the tiny package

which was the Creator of the Universe

to her breast and shoulder,

so that Its eyes looked toward the door.

It saw a sun,

which was Its mother's shoulder,

and then the moon of the midwife,

and then a star,

which was Joseph at the doorway

with the lamp.

A shepherd told Joseph
that they had come to adore the baby,
who was the Creator of the Universe.
The shepherds did not wish to crowd into the stable.
They meant to kneel in the courtyard,
if only the child could be brought for a moment
to the door.
The child was brought to the door by Joseph.
The real Christmas star had then set.
The real moon had set.
It was near dawn.
The Creator's eyes could not focus
on the myriad pinpricks
which were all the other heavenly bodies,
nor the sheep.
The Creator could see only
the torches out there.

But then,
when Joseph carried the swaddled baby
back to the manger,
one torchbearer came after him,
followed by two other men.
These were three wise men,
sent by King Herod from Jerusalem
to find this child.
Herod said he wished to worship it.
He really wished to kill it,
for it was supposed to be
a new King of the Jews.
The torch was held close to the baby,
between Mary and the midwife,
so that the wise men
could see what manner of baby this
was.

The Creator
now saw a sun,
a moon
and a star
come together
in an impossible cosmic tangle.
What could be the explanation?
The baby's eyes had crossed.

So It closed Its eyes
and saw orange—
because of the torch nearby.
It heard the wise men
prove they were truly wise.
They told Mary and Joseph
that this was the Creator of the Universe
they saw,
and that they would
not tell the King or anyone
of Its birth.
They made presents
of such small treasures
as they happened to have with them.
They left.

When the Creator opened Its eyes again,
they were still crossed.
Joseph's lamp and the midwife
looked like this
to It.

But Its eyes uncrossed in sleep—

And during a dream of Its Mother—
never to cross again.

A rooster crowed,
but the Creator of the Universe
slept on and on.
Joseph picked It up,
and still It slept on and on.
Joseph carried It out of doors.
It dreamed purple.
Heat baked Its face.

It opened Its eyes.
It saw what It thought was a sun.
For the first time in Its short human life
It was right:
It really was
a sun It saw—
a small one.
And an ox was led out of the stable
to plow,
and an ass was led out of the stable
to carry firewood.
A rooster crowed again,
although the sun had been up for hours.
And life went on.

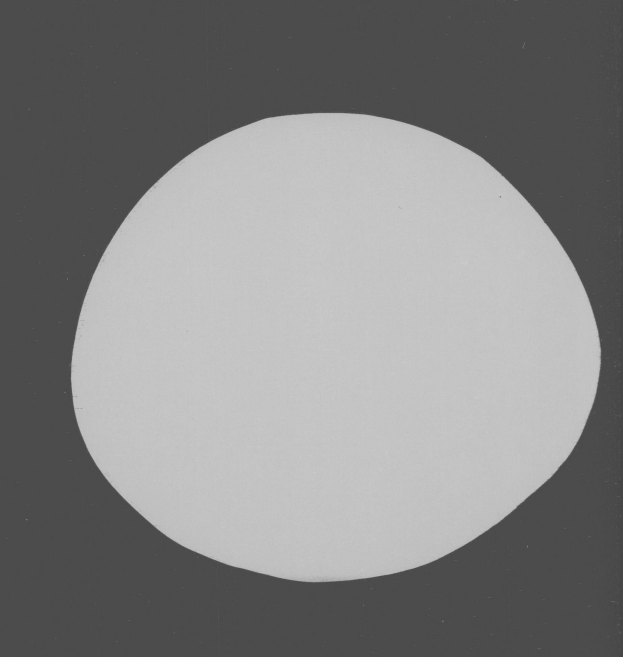

Amen.